Fly On

Dr. Omkar Bhatkar

Ukiyoto Publishing

All global publishing rights are held by

Ukiyoto Publishing

Published in 2023

Content Copyright © Dr. Omkar Bhatkar

ISBN 9789360490416

All rights reserved.
No part of this publication may be reproduced,
transmitted, or stored in a retrieval system, in any
form by any means, electronic, mechanical,
photocopying, recording or otherwise, without the
prior permission of the publisher.

The moral rights of the author have been asserted.

This is a work of fiction. Names, characters, businesses,
places, events, locales, and incidents are either the
products of the author's imagination or used in a
fictitious manner. Any resemblance to actual persons,
living or dead, or actual events is purely coincidental.

This book is sold subject to the condition that it shall
not by way of trade or otherwise, be lent, resold, hired
out or otherwise circulated, without the publisher's
prior consent, in any form of binding or cover other
than that in which it is published.

www.ukiyoto.com

Dedicated to

Mark Aumoine
Prachi Sarmalkar
Harsh Shah
Balarama Fornes
Sanket Angane
Pedro Magalhães
Nitya Narasimhan

Characters

Sarthak

Sarthak is about 30 years old carefree and easygoing man, still in between boyhood and manhood. Travelling from Goa to Ahmedabad on a sleeper bus which goes via Mumbai. Sarthak might have been a lot of things as far as his characteristics are concerned, but the play is about this bus journey and what we see on the bus journey is also another side of him. There are new discoveries about himself which also leaves him with a renewed 'Sarthak'. He dresses in loose and bright clothes and walks as if he is a model on the streets. He is an unmissable character wherever he is be it a room, park, bus or petrol pump station.

Farhan

Farhan is an easily missable character on the street for his boy next door mannerisms and features. Farhan dresses in comfortable clothes and takes life very seriously, he is disciplined and talks less. Although, on this journey, he surprises himself when he meets Sarthak. Farhan is an avid reader and likes to spend time all by himself. He is travelling on a sleeper bus from Goa to Mumbai.

Both of them discover each other on this journey and nothing remains the same after that.

The play premiered in Mumbai at Marathi Sahitya Sangh in 2017, Directed by Dr. Omkar Bhatkar, Sarthak was played by Harsh Shah and Farhan was played by Omkar Bhatkar. Later shows were essayed by Abhishek and Omkar.

Writer-Director Note

Fly On is a journey of one night, loosely based on a real-life incident. The destinations can be changed depending on the geography where the play is staged. The stage design is minimal, evocative blue lights can be used effectively to enhance the scenes. The most crucial part of this play is its casting. A play like Fly On….. requires a delicate choice of two characters who can imbibe the traits and emotional vulnerability of Sarthak and Farhan. The play doesn't need a break, however, can be included depending on the director's decision. The play prefers being not boxed in identity politics and labels and Fly on….. is an attempt to tell a story devoid of any tags and labelling. The play would be restricted in movements since most parts of the play are located on the bus. Only use movements when the characters move out of the bus. Emphasis can be laid on performance and dialogues. The play if staged can be accompanied by lilting acoustic guitar (Live or pre-recorded) for emotional sequences and blackouts.

The songs mentioned in the play are suggestive, the Director is free to choose music of their choice or even use live music to accompany the play.

For public performances and staging of the play kindly get in touch on

metamorphosistheatreinc@gmail.com

From The Critics Column

Life is a journey and the people coming to you are all strangers. Still, you fall in love with some of them. True love is unconditional and is far more intense than a "give and take" relationship. True love knows no barriers of caste, creed, religion or nationality is well known. Though here it goes beyond that and enters an unchartered terrain of social universe. You may have your reservations but this play travels unhindered in the realm of love where a human being is just a human without any compunction of gender. The two men reveal themselves before each other and find themselves in a tight grip of love. Though the bus journey ends at its destination it's not the end of man-to-man love which continues in memories.

Based on a real experience of someone's life it is a story of a bus journey. Farhan an introvert meets his co-passenger who seems to be talkative and extrovert. As the journey is long Farhan accepts his gesture of friendliness. Soon it is revealed that the guy has come just out of jail after partial remission of his long term because of his minor crime of drug peddling. Very emotively he explains how he spent the torturing period of three months. Farhan feels sympathy for him and so comes nearer to the console. Soon, both are under emotional tide and a full-fledged love evolves. The love that is has overt physical ramifications too. The whole play is embedded with the philosophical dialogues uttered by Farhan who is often in a contemplative mood. Baffled on each of them is his newly found friend, a jaunty youth. The chemistry goes well because in spite of all the paradoxes, there is a basic similarity. Both want to do things differently. Both of them abhor treading the beaten track.

Where Farhan likes to be lost in the books and flies in the poetic thoughts his friend tries everything from smoking to drugs occasionally. Both seem to be cut from their outer worlds at the sentimental level and a great void exists in their respective lives. Now, both the voids converge with each other breaking the social barriers to fill them up. As per an allegorical dialogue, the internal void of a person matches the immense void of the sea and a poem is generated. Though the love between these two men is unprepared and random but is unconditional and true. Both of them know they will never meet again but the experience they had will remain forever.

The script does not seek to tell you a story rather it takes you to a platform where you are able to mull over the hidden things taking it in broad light under an open sky. Writer -Director Dr. Bhatkar has brilliantly put the narrative on stage. Long scenes on a single bus seat might have been challenging for an average director but Omkar made it so natural that you can't even appreciate the probable brainstorming behind it. The seat was shown with the help of a big bench and the black curtains framing over it. Hundreds of paper geese were hanging from the ceiling all over the stage and feathers were blue-coloured signifying the colour of the open sky. This pragmatic innovation helped in creating a philosophical ambiance.

By Hemant Das
Stage Critic

Contents

Scene I The Wait For The Bus	1
Scene II Moving Onto The Bus	3
Scene III The Bus Halts For Dinner	11
Scene IV The Bus Moves After Dinner	20
Scene V The Bus Breaks Down At Midnight	36
Scene VI The Dawn	39
Scene VII The Tinted Glass	42
About the Author	*44*

Scene I
The Wait For The Bus

It's 5:30 in the evening and there is a boy who is waiting for his bus. He has been on holiday alone and now it's time for him to return to his usual life. He is waiting for his bus which is about to come at 6 o'clock. He doesn't see many people at the bus stand but he is used to this bus stand and he also knows the bus is usually late. There he sees another young boy - Sarthak walking with his beard, his piercing, and a tattoo on the skin; like a typical hippy-like carefree who has been to Goa And he has loads of luggage. So we have Sarthak who has been to Goa for a holiday for a month, an Indian-American by origin waiting at the bus stop not knowing what has happened to his bus. It's already a quarter past six. Like a directionless person, he walks up to Farhan and asks Farhan if he can help him out with this bus ticket he has.

Sarthak :

Can you help me with the bus ticket?

Farhan :

Don't you have a phone? Because, usually they update you for buses running late".

Sarthak :

My phone got stolen in Goa. I was having my dinner alone when I got up to pick up the oregano bottle from another table, and the moment I turned back, my phone was gone.

Farhan :

Welcome to Goa.

Farhan :

Where are you going?

Sarthak :

I'm going to Ahmedabad.

Farhan :

Oh! I'm going to Mumbai. But I believe it's the same bus. It must be going to Ahmedabad via Mumbai.

Farhan :

(out of curiosity or just to keep the conversation going) What's your seat number?

Sarthak :

16.

Farhan :

(looking at his ticket) Oh! Mine is 15. So, you're right one berth behind me.

Scene II
Moving Onto The Bus

(That's how they spoke for some time. They spoke about where they were living, and their reason for the trip for a brief time till the bus came. YES! The bus comes in. The bus is late but it's there. They both get into the bus. 15 is a lower berth and 16 is an upper berth)

Sarthak :

Oh! I'm on top of you.

(He then goes to his upper berth at 16 and Farhan sits at his berth at 15. There begins a journey. A journey that would possibly leave them changed after this night. A journey that they'd never expect to change the course of their lives or a journey like other journeys where people get in at a stop, spend some time with each other and get out when their stop comes. Maybe this is a perfect analogy of how people walk in your life and people walk out of your life. The bus journey from Mapusa to Mumbai.)

(Farhan was sitting quietly. He settled himself, put his slippers into a tray, kept the water bottle in a case, kept the bag in a corner, took out his phone charger and put it in a socket to see if the socket was working. Like many private buses, they don't often work and then he was curious to see if the small little reading light was working. The reading light usually does not work either. He switched off the light viola. He switched it on and it didn't work. This night was a night he didn't want to hear music but he wanted to complete his incomplete book by

Murakami that he was reading. But there was no light and for a moment he just looked up and asked Sarthak)

Farhan :

Do you mind? Can you just check if your reading light is working?

(He doesn't know what light Sarthak is talking about?)

Sarthak :

What light?

Farhan :

The reading light!

(The reading light at Sarthak's berth wasn't working either)

Farhan :

As usual there isn't anything new to this. The reading light just works when the buses are new for a month and then they just go off to plunge into eternal darkness.

(Farhan was disappointed as he could not read anymore at night)

Sarthak :

Are you planning to read something? What is it?

Farhan :

It is The Wind-Up Bird Chronicle.

Sarthak :

What is it about?

Farhan :

It's a story about a man who lives a not-so-perfect life with his wife. But what happens one day when the cat they got when they were married, disappears and he starts looking for it. What happens in the search for the cat, is that his wife disappears and what happens when he goes down into a well that does not have water? What happens to his life when he realizes his wife disappears from his life for no reason? I don't know further because I'm still halfway.......

Some time passes and Sarthak looks down

Sarthak :

Hey, do you want to see something?

Farhan :

What?

Sarthak :

It's a bag full of coins from different places.

Farhan :

I don't mind. Is it okay if I see it down or do you want me to come up and see it with you?

(To which there's a sweet smile on Sarthak's face and he says)

Sarthak :

Yeah, I can trust you.

(What happens in the spur of a moment in Farhan's mind is how can a stranger with a gentle smile just say "I can trust you" who hardly knows him for not more than 20 lines?

So here Sarthak gives the coins down to the lower Berth and he opens up the coins. He takes them out and they're from different places from Ireland to the UK to UAE to Kuwait to different places. And in that moment Sarthak comes down from his berth)

Sarthak :

I can help you with places you don't know where they belong to.

(This way begins a conversation that travels from Ireland to the UK, from UAE to the US, from Thailand to Bali, from Monarchy to Socialism as they start talking about countries, currencies and denominators. After they discuss the coins, Farhan closes the pouch and gives it back to Sarthak. And the one question he asks is:)

Farhan :

Why are these coins in your bag while travelling? Why isn't it in your home?

Sarthak :

I carried it by mistake. It was at my father's place.

Farhan smiles in his mind and thinks "How could somebody make a mistake like that? Of carrying coins"

Farhan :

What were you doing in Arambol? Where were you staying?

Sarthak :

I was here for a month-long holiday. Just wanted to get away from everything. Just wanted to be a free bird. I have a lot in my life and I just want to get over it.

I work in the postal services in the US in the Lost and Found Department which is about tracing letters and documents which do not have proper addresses. Then tracing and sending it either to the sender or the person to whom it's to be delivered.

Farhan :

Sounds fascinating!

Sarthak :

It's not as fascinating as you think it is. It's a damn boring Job!

Farhan :

Really? But letter writing excites me.

Sarthak :

It's nothing like letter writing. It's just official documents. People no longer write letters.

Farhan :

That's true. People no longer write letters. I love letter Writing. I still write letters. Letters are so tender, the excitement that the letter holds when the post person hands over to you. The compassionate curiosity of who could have sent it and the world that changes after opening the envelope, not literally that the world changes but that letter holding the capacity to take you to deep sleep or make you sleep less. How everything in that moment stands stranded, life in that one piece of paper.

Sarthak :

Yes, that's very true. But my job is very boring. What do you do Farhan?

Farhan :

Me? I do many things. I like to write, though I haven't written anything considerable yet just a few short stories and poems.

Sarthak :

Oh that sounds exciting! I have a friend whom I met in Arambol and this person was from Germany and he used to come to the beach and just write and write. So, every day he would write; like a page or two by evening and he just kept it, no specific agenda, no specific topic.

Farhan :

Yes, writing is just like that. I love looking at the sea and writing.

Sarthak :

Why only the sea?

Farhan :

I don't know, somehow the sea and even the sky are two elements, when you look into them, they look into your eyes and they reach right down to your heart and they strike a chord with your heart in such a way that you connect to it by disconnecting the world.

Sky and the Sea are these large expanses, infinities that make you realize what you are in this larger universe. A mere speck of dust and what else? Your existence, your inexistence, happiness, your joy, your everything is merely a speck of dust. Does it mean anything in the larger universe? Nothing! And that nothingness opens up the void in you.

Sarthak :

Can I see some of your written work sometimes?

Farhan :

Yes, of course, I can send it to you once I reach Bombay and maybe when we stop for a break, I can read out to you, some of my poems.

Sarthak :

Hey….! That sounds amazing. You know, I have never written anything. I write and I try my best at it. I mean I write articles, official articles. I've never been able to write a poem. I don't even know if I can write a poem, I'm sure it will be a bad poem of life if I ever try.

Farhan :

There is nothing like Good or Bad poetry. Either it is good poetry or it is not just poetry, and poetry isn't about writing. Poetry is something that happens; it unveils to you. You don't have to sit down to write a poem. A poem lifts the veil and opens up to you like a bud that slowly opens up and transforms into a flower. That's what poetry is. It just happens. You don't sit down to write a poem, the poem writes itself if the one holding the pen has a heart that's just open and I'm sure one day Sarthak, you too will be able to write your poem. Just plunge into the flow when it happens.

Lights dim to blue

Scene III
The Bus Halts For Dinner

The bus stops for 20 minutes and both of them go for dinner. It's a cool blue night. The wind is blowing. It creates a hauling sound as it passes through the bamboo plantations in the forests. A quiet little dinner place but none of them want to have dinner as they don't like to eat while traveling so they just have tea. While Farhan is drinking his tea, Sarthak lights a cigarette and takes a puff. On the cold blue night, the cigarette smoke mixes with the already hazy atmosphere and it looks as if only both of them exist in that haziness around and nobody else and they start talking,

Sarthak :

Do you smoke?

Farhan :

No, I don't.

Sarthak :

So, don't you have any addictions?

Farhan :

Well, my only addiction is reading. I read, I read and I read and I can't do without it. I think the day I stopped reading I would go mad. I can't live without it. It makes living possible. Reading is something that just transforms you. Like if you read Murakami or Kundera, time stops. Of course, I read them in translation and they drive me crazy. I love translations because you can learn so much from these world authors which you otherwise never get to know.

Sarthak :

Yeah man! I never heard these names like Murakami

Farhan :

I'm sure that you're pretending

Sarthak :

Why would I, I'm not pulling your leg. My life doesn't offer me that circle in which I can remain in touch with reading and authors.

Farhan :

I see, Then there's Han Kang. I love Han Kang. She's a Korean writer.

Sarthak :

So, what does she write about? Or all of them?

Farhan :

Well, they write about life, what else? But you should read one of their books. It's just mind-blowing, you know! After you finish even a Murakami book, you feel like you're no longer the same person. There is something about you that changes and it transforms you. It's so fascinating what a book can do to you! And when that happens I call it my intellectual orgasm.haha..

Sarthak :

Nice. That's a great addiction.

Farhan :

Yeah, it's great. Makes life worth living.

Sarthak :

So, have you done drugs?

Farhan :

Not really. I'm wary of the concept of an external substance that takes you to an altered state of consciousness. To me, if a piece of poetry or a piece of art or a piece of literature can just take you mentally high, then I don't think I need something like drugs.

Sarthak :

But drugs are different. You can't compare both and that's a different zone. You're just shot up in your brain and you're in a different reality.

Farhan :

Yeah, they must be but I'm still worried about it and meditation is again great too.

Sarthak :

Yeah! No doubt about it. Meditation is great but still from what a drug can give you, meditation is very different. It can't give you that. It can't alter your state of consciousness. Of course, even meditation can but not at the level that drugs can.......

Sarthak :

Well, I haven't asked you, but, what have you studied, Farhan?

Farhan :

Well, Well, Well, I find that complicated to answer. I don't relate to only formal education as a form of learning. But to the answer in the convential way, I have completed my master's in Anthropology and I love to read about cultures and civilizations.

Sarthak :

Anthropology, really great indeed. So, what's your favorite book?

Farhan :

I don't think I can have one favorite book, Sarthak, there are so many, so many authors that I love. There are *just* so many. Whether you take Oscar Wilde, whether you take Kafka or Mishima or even Gabriel Garcia Marquez. There are just too many writers that I love. I can't pick up one writer that I love. Almost impossible.

Sarthak :

I wish I could read like you man, you read a lot.

Farhan :

Even I could say I do wish something's like you. Like something…….

Sarthak :

What do you mean? I just know a little bit of music and that is it.

Farhan :

Exactly! Music! I'm not gifted with musical hands to play any musical instruments. I have no voice that can sing. I mean I wish I could.

As a child, you know I always wished I could learn the violin but that day never came and I have never learnt it but I'm sure one day I will be able to do so.

Sarthak :

Why are you waiting for one day? You can just do it once you go back to Mumbai.

Farhan :

Well, we can say that. But, you will be back tomorrow in Ahmedabad. I will be in Bombay and that's it. We will be sucked up in the routine of life. The violin will just be a part of a dream that I sleep and dream about until I make time for the violin. But I will make it one day. I saw that you were carrying a violin or something…

Sarthak :

Oh that? That's a ukulele.

Farhan :

Oh, So you play the Ukulele?

Sarthak :

Yes, I just bought it in Goa. Because I had nothing to play so bought this Ukulele.

Farhan :

Wow! It's marvelous. You know why I love the violin; because I love its shape. And I love the sound of it. The ukulele has the exact shape, I recently saw someone play it and I thought. If Violin is going to take a lot of time, maybe I should just start with Ukulele.

Sarthak :

I can give you my Ukulele.

Farhan :

Are you crazy?

Sarthak :

Yeah, I can give it to you. I have one at home that is very good. I can give this to you. You can use it.

Farhan :

Are you serious?

Sarthak :

Yeah, of course, you can take my ukulele. It's right up on the berth. You can take it in the morning. I'm totally fine with it.

Farhan :

Ahhhh! Coincidence can't be so coincidental that I end up seeing a man carrying a ukulele, and I crave to play the Ukulele. And look at this now, I have someone giving me a Ukulele right under the blue moon in this Hauling sound of breeze right on this foggy night. How can anything be so magical? This is

Magic. What a coincidence. Coincidence can't be so coincidental.

Sarthak :

So, you do believe in coincidences? Like destiny?

Farhan :

Destiny? I really don't know. I think we carve out our destiny. There is nothing that is predestined. All you need is the will to turn the world upside down. Like this ukulele... maybe I truly wanted it and see how it came from *I don't know* where. I mean look at us. Two strangers. I've never had a conversation like this with someone I met on a bus or a train and look how we are talking? As if we knew each other for *I don't know how long'*. I mean we never share so many intimate details with someone you just met, which I am doing and feeling so comfortable. I never felt so comfortable with some stranger.

Sarthak :

That's true man. You know, like I went to the toilet and... then you just followed in to pee. Farhan, you'd just find it weird but, I don't like to pee with people around. so I use the cubicles. But you know when you walked in and you were peeing as I was peeing, we were talking while peeing. And for the first time in my life, I felt so comfortable talking to somebody while peeing. It is something that I have never done and have told nobody about.

Farhan :

Are you also like that? I am also uncomfortable peeing with people around. Like when I go to malls or theatres, I don't like when too many people are around when I am peeing. I wait till there are fewer people and I prefer using cubicles. It's very strange, you know. I never wanted to pee but then I thought it's a long bus journey so it's better peeing and when I was talking to you, I suddenly thought in my mind because *I'm a man of etiquette*. I was like, "Is it good to talk while you're peeing" and for a moment I was like "Would you shut up Farhan!" and I was just talking and I felt absolutely comfortable. It's very strange though. I've never felt so comfortable next to a man while peeing. I don't know how both of us sometimes come on the same page. Talk about the same thing?

Sarthak :

Don't think my idea of coincidence is like you! Like, I don't think there's something like coincidence happening. There's nothing like destiny, like Coincidence. I don't know how to put it man but, I just don't think it is a coincidence.

Farhan :

I believe so. Everything happens for a reason. I don't know. It will have some meaning in the larger picture of life. Maybe we can't see it but I'm sure there's a purpose. I don't think it's just a ukulele I had to receive on a journey if that was the case; it could have happened this way also, it's happening this way, like this. There must be a reason; I believe there's some reason behind everything possible.

Lights dim to blue

Scene IV
The Bus Moves After Dinner

Bus starts moving. They both sit at berth number 15 and continue the conversation.

Farhan :

So how long have you been in India, Sarthak? And when will you be going back?

Sarthak :

It's a long story, man. I don't know how to say it. Actually...... I was in jail. I was in jail for the last 6 months in Al Wathba in Abu Dhabi. It's a long story. It's just a fuck... fuck.. fucking story! It screwed up my life. Everything that I had. The hair that you see on my head now, was gone. I was shaved off, bald. That one fucking blanket that they used to give me. I used to sleep in that veranda in that extreme heat of 40 degrees Celsius. The clothes they gave me were rags, mere rags dirty with soil and they didn't ask about the food. I lost 30 kgs in the first two months; that I was there. Stale fish, stale meat is what they used to give. I vomited out in the first few weeks. I couldn't have it and I stopped eating. But that wasn't helping. I had no connections. I didn't know what the fuck was I doing in that place and if I tell you why, you'd wonder about the cruelty of life.

I was slightly high when I got down at the airport. I had a connecting flight to the US. I was traveling via Etihad Airlines. Fucking security of airlines Etihad… I would never want to travel with them. I never ever want to go by them. I don't know how they're promoting it so much online. I was high when I was on the flight but I made sure that whatever I had in my bag was thrown out as far as any substance was concerned. When I got down, they asked me to come aside for checking. They are watchdogs, whenever they see someone a little different, a little high or something, they take them aside for checking. I said "Okay". They checked me up and down literally. They didn't find anything. They opened up my bag and they began checking a little… little… little…. Everything inch by inch. They didn't find anything. Somehow later, they went into the penholder in my bag and they found this little piece of Hashish not even the size of my thumb. They said,

"Come, we will take you"

I asked "For what?"

"We have to take you. You are carrying Hashish in Abu Dhabi."

I said "But that's not even ...."

They weren't ready to listen. Such fucking bastards! They went to the corners of my bag and removed everything possible. Of Course, they didn't find anything, just bits and scraps of tobacco here and there of the role of a joint and put it all together and they showed it in a document that I was smuggling drugs. For a moment I didn't know what happened to me. They handcuffed me and threw me in jail. There I was going to the US to resume my job and here I am landing in jail and for what? I just didn't know. Rules in the Middle East are totally fucked up. They are all against Hashish. Apparently, it was the Sheikh's son who died with an overdose of Hashish and so they've banned it in the whole country and banned it everywhere. Any consumption of drugs is illegal. It's just a fucked up country. The laws are just fucked up. They didn't give me a chance to say anything. They didn't let me say anything. The document they produced was in Arabic. How was I supposed to even read it? You don't know Farhan what I was going through. It was screwed up. You know there was no place to walk in the jail. People were sleeping left and right. You'd have to make your place slouching in a corner or somewhere. I was stinking. I was beaten in the jail. It took me some time. After three months, I somehow made friends in prison and one of them was closely related to the Sheikh. He told me about a lot of secrets about the Sheikh family. I appealed and my appeal was denied. I couldn't talk to my family. My brother was there but he suffers from extreme bipolarities. My mother is not here. She lives in the UK. Father is all alone. He couldn't do anything either. Not one human had noticed that I was gone. I could even disappear from the face of the earth and the world would go on moving without the slightest hiccup. Things were tremendously complicated, to be sure, but one thing was clear 'No one needed me'

The laws in UAE are just fucked up. No one could do anything. Azir is the friend from the Sheikh's family who said things in your case might get a little easier. It was then after 6 months I was released out of jail. My sentence was supposed to be for 2 years. I was released in 6 months. Azir told me that there is something called the Mohram in which the prime minister has the authority to forgive the sinners in jail and those who have come on their smaller sins are forgiven. So, in 6 months, I was the one who was led out of jail. But those 6 months had destroyed my life, my being and my existence. How am I going to go back to my job? How am I going to answer them? Where was I? Who will believe my story? And what all happened in the six months? Did I disappear on the flight, never to be found again? And what was me now, how much was it really 'me'?

Am I really who I was or is there something about me that got killed in that jail? When I got that document of the sentence and I showed it to my lawyer, they told me that I was carrying 5 different types of drugs. It said I was carrying 5 different kinds of drugs. The amazing part in all the different parts, Hashish was not once mentioned. So what was carrying wasn't mentioned and all I was not carrying was not mentioned. I can't do anything about it. At the most, I can write an article or a book. Because I know many such people in jail who were there for no such reason.

Some stories were more horrendous than mine. One could just cry listening to them or think of the fragility or the impossibility of living a life. It is indeed an unbearable lightness to be alive. Such stories that existed in the jail for people, who were not supposed to be there, were there. Such great souls were all damaged in that cell, and it was then I decided to just come to Goa and unwind myself. And I think I had a good time. I met interesting people, made some music, and had interesting conversations.

While they were talking for such a long time on the bus, it became dark. The lights are switched off, the curtains are put and since Sarthak is still talking about his story, it becomes very important for them to sit close and talk so they do not disturb the others while talking, and when Sarthak has tears in his eyes, his hair standing at its end on his body as he was talking about that jail. It was that moment Farhan held Sarthak's hand. It was at that moment when Sarthak rested his face on Farhan's shoulders. It was at that moment that they kissed each other. It was a slow kiss. Slow..it was a gentle kiss, very very gentle like two fragile souls trying to hold each other with their fragility making sure that even the holding of each other was so tender that they didn't hurt each other. Their firmness would kill what they were holding. Therefore they were holding it tenderly, delicately as if they both were made of glass. Fragile glass can be broken away even by a blow or a breeze. They look into each other's eyes and Farhan says nothing. There is a long silence.

Sarthak :

I didn't imagine that…..

Sarthak :

The mistakes I'd committed, maybe they were part of my very makeup, an inescapable part of my being. I couldn't do without them.

Sarthak :

Did I not know that my approach is off-tangent? Of Course, I do, but it's the 'off tangent' approach that appeals to me. I do not want to be answerable. I didn't want to behave in a measured way. I do not want to be reasonable. I admire my passion, knowing that passion is excessive. Intoxicated, I do not want to emerge from Intoxication. Now, tell me something about your life Farhan. Tell me something more about you.

Farhan :

I don't have so much to say as you are saying about your story that just happened. Yeah, I do have a life but you will discover me with time.

Sarthak :

With time? This bus journey will end by morning.

Farhan :

I hope you'll stay in touch.

Sarthak :

Of course, I'll stay in touch. You can right away send me a Facebook request. I don't have a number. I can't give it to you right now. But you can send me a request right away. Look for me. I'm hugging a tree in the picture.

They both were silent for some time. In that moment,

Farhan :

Look outside! The moon is shining so beautifully.

The moon was blue which they can see from the tinted blue grass. They could see how the bus was moving fast and how the moon was moving fast with it. It was that hour of the night when once again they held their hands, clashed with each other and this time they kissed much more firmly. As the lips parted, Sarthak opened his eyes and very slowly said,

Sarthak :

Thank you for taking me to where I hadn't been in such a long time. Where you have taken me in a moment, I had yearned for it for a long time. Every night, every day, the time I spend in my room, I wish there was someone. Someone who would take care, someone who would just care, just be around to make you feel less alone. You know I was in Arambol and there were these two brothers. Despite being brothers, they didn't share a room because they said they couldn't stand each other.

Farhan :

Yeah, that's okay. I don't share my space with my brother. It's not important that you need to share space. It troubles me when I have somebody in my space. I need my space. I need my room to myself.

Sarthak :

Yeah, you're right. But, you know, it's not the day but it's the evening. The moment the sun goes down, its evening, and there is a loneliness that creeps into your house through your doors, through your windows, through the crevices of your walls and they tell you, "Look, You're alone. Look, you have no one. Look, what you are going to do now?" And that loneliness hangs in the air throughout the night and you wish only there was someone to hold you tight at that moment, close to your heart and make you feel life is less lonesome and beautiful

As the night fades and as the day brightens, the warmth of the sun fills the house and then you wish Let it be, that's how life is... Maybe that is the reason why you look at many Hindi songs and even English ones. This is why many of them dramatize the nights. I guess this is why the night makes you feel the void of life, the nothingness of life. It is a darkness that makes you realize "Look, you're a mere fleeting speck of dust and there's no one who really loves you.

Long pause, they look at each other and outside and back at each other.

Farhan :

I like to look at you, your eyes look so deep, and your lips are like .... I don't know when was it that I kissed like this, you are just beautiful!

I don't know what to say, Sarthak, we have both been in love, I have been in love, I don't know what to call this is this Love or story of one night, which will pass as soon as the sun is out. I don't know whether we will be in touch when you go to Ahmedabad, I know myself. We all are so unpredictable, of course I would like to be in touch, I don't know what is the story of this night. But I like to be in the moment, I don't know whether this is love or the reason why we met. I am sure you must have seen what was written in front of the bus, 'Jesus will show the way' Maybe Jesus is showing us the way. This is the way I don't know when this will end, but as far as I know about life.

Sometimes things just happen in retrospect. Sometimes things just happen, one event, followed by another and........and these events are like dots in the vast space outside.

Events are random situations but as Human beings, we like to make sense of chaos. We like to look at things as coincidences, we do not like to see things in chaos, and everything looks more meaningful to us like a picture connecting dots, maybe that's how it's supposed to be. One dot here, one situation. Another dot there, another situation and a third dot there, third situation, and such many more situations scattered like dots. Of course, they are randomly scattered and don't make sense. Therefore, somehow, we try to connect a dot to another and furthermore. So that we could make sense of situations and present a picture to ourselves and maybe label it as a 'Coincidence'. Maybe, I'm not sure about it, But I've thought about it even this way. Sarthak, maybe it's like a route that has no meaning in itself, its meaning derives entirely from two points that it connects.

You might be wondering what am I blabbering!

Sarthak :

I have never met someone like this and spoken to them for hours. When was the last time I spoke to someone like this? I don't know. I am so glad I met you. I don't know what would happen if I did not meet you.

Sarthak :

I am going to lie down a bit. Farhan, I just think I need some sleep. I did not sleep last night.

(Farhan was a bit shaken, he couldn't make sense of the situation. He doesn't understand why Sarthak wants to go to his berth now)

Sarthak :

Or Farhan, should I go up?

Farhan :

Whatever you feel like.

Sarthak :

Then, I shall go up.

Sarthak :

Can you wake me up? How should I put it? Can you wake me up till the next stop comes so that I can come down and we can talk more?

Farhan :

Yeah, I can do that; the next stop will be in an hour or two. I'll wake you up

Sarthak climbs up and goes up, they close the curtains and the pale blue moonlight falls on their face.

Sarthak :

(these are thoughts- talking to himself) Why did he go up? Was he really tired? Should I wake him up? Will I sound desperate? What if he isn't a light sleeper? Or should I push him and wake him up if he does not get up? That might be rude. Why all of this, and now how will I survive this

Farhan kept on thinking; the AC of the bus made it chill, and he tried to make himself warm in every possible way. And somehow he manages, after some time the bus stops and he gets happy, and does not know how to wake up a stranger like this. So he saw his ankle and ticked it a little. Sarthak moves his head and looks at Farhan but his eyes are still closed and Farhan gets disappointed he thought he really might want to sleep, he is tired, or he does not want to talk anymore but why would that happen? Was it the kiss?

Sarthak :

(these are thoughts- talking to himself) What was it, this berth is so big for a tiny person like me, I am just rolling from one end to the other, though the berth is meant for just one person it was so comfortable with him, now when he is not there it feels empty, I don't know how to fill it up.

Farhan :

(these are thoughts- talking to himself) I had constructed a taller, defensive wall around me. Maybe even Sarthak has built a wall, and maybe that's why he doesn't wish to come down and talk. Maybe he wants to protect himself and stay in that wall around him. What remained behind the wall though was much the same as what lay behind me. And yet we were isolated in our own walls.

Sarthak :

(these are thoughts- talking to himself) like me, is he a fragile soul trapped in a glass bottle?

Farhan :

(these are thoughts- talking to himself) He wanted me then. His heart was open to me. Yet, I held myself back, back on the surface of the berth. I was glued to the berth and he was floating on the stars outside. His life was flowing outside and I was stuck in the lifeless bus. And in the end, he left me and my life was lost all over again. And I'm now freezing in this coldness, maybe I should really go down.

(While thinking and looking at the night, Sarthak comes down)

Sarthak :

It's damn cold man, I can't sleep like this. I don't like AC

Farhan :

I too hate AC, do you want to lie down here

Sarthak :

Anyway !! It was so stupid to go up.

Sarthak :

I was tired. I wanted to sleep but I wanted to talk to you too. Why did I do that man?

Sarthak makes some space down and they both lie down, holding hands of each other. Few moments of silence, then looking into each other's eyes.

Farhan :

Have you ever been with a man?

Sathak :

Not at least in the last 30 years. No, never. Just something with a guy in boarding school, you know how it is in boarding, just a little something and then it got over in some time. Later I just had women in my life, all sorts of women. I have a girlfriend now but I am not sure, as it is very confusing as she was engaged sometime back. She is a radiologist. We are good with each other but she has a friend Samantha. She likes her too. So, she loves me and her, and I don't know how to talk about her; she does not know what to do. That's why I don't know whether she is my girlfriend or not.

Also there, was another girl Alice; we were together for quite some time. She was smart and outgoing but after spending a year in a relationship, we too moved away from each other. We were always together and spent every day together. Slowly it all faded into oblivion. She was living beneath a sky that had nothing to do with me. She no longer sought me out, I no longer sought her out. Recalling her now awakens neither love nor hatred. At the thought of her, I am as if... anaesthetized with no ideas, no emotion.

What about you Farhan, are you bisexual?

Farhan :

How to answer that Sarthak,

Farhan :

Let us try by looking at you, you never actually have been with a man in 35 years, and this is the first man you have been so intimate with a man, now do you think yourself gay, or is it just about something that happened in one night? Is it something only about the physical? Will such a thing never happen? If it does, will it be only physical? At the moment is it only physical?

Sarthak :

(softly) No

Farhan :

It's not just physical attraction but something beyond, something beyond that invokes parts of us unknown to us.

Sarthak :

I like you because of how you talk to someone who speaks like this, someone with such a beautiful heart.

Farhan :

Exactly it's what they are, call them what you want, it's what is in the mind, it's about how they like each other, the way you hold me and I hold you right now so delicately like if they stumble, they will break, at this moment, but I don't want to lose you but I know you will be gone, I want to hold you so tight so that I can take a part of you with me. You are wearing my T-shirt, might be helping you from the cold. And you know when you went up what I did, I smelt my own breath and I could smell you in my breath. I wanted to keep this forever. And all this is momentary. This will be nothing in the morning.

They both lay in each other's arms and fell asleep in the darkened night.

Music - Stars Die by Porcupine can be played here from the first few stanzas until the scenes fade to the next.

Sarthak :

(these are thoughts and he is talking to himself) How much of this person I called myself was actually 'me' in this moment and how much was 'not'? These hands holding Farhan's and how much percentage of them would I call my own? The bus journey, the berth, the glittering glow of the stars in the sky and the darkened road around, how much of it is real? How much of what I experienced with Farhan is actually 'me'? What I felt, I've never felt for another

man! Then what is true? Was I not aware of a whole existence of mine that I've just realized on this journey? Am I an unknown self to myself? Did it take me 36 years to also know another deep side of me? How much of this person I called myself was actually 'me' in this moment and how much was 'not'?

The more I thought about it, the less I seemed to understand.

Farhan :

(these are thoughts and he is talking to himself) Because everyone is seeking the same thing: an imaginary place, their own castle in the air and their very own special corner of it. Maybe I'm seeking this imaginary safe place, maybe Sarthak is too. Maybe that's why we are holding each other so tight so that this moment won't pass, where we have found our safe haven.

Lights dim to blue

Scene V
The Bus Breaks Down At Midnight

The bus faints and is halting for a long time, Sarthak opens the curtains and sees the bus has broken down.

They step outside and they see the sky full of stars shining bright.

Sarthak :

You know I love star gazing. There was this, one night that I spent in Sanjan and it was an out worldly experience. I was awake till 8 in the morning and I saw 14-15 shooting stars in one night. When I saw them falling down that night, I knew no one would believe me the next morning. Stars tumbling down, to become nothing, destroying their beauty by burning themselves to death.

That was one beautiful night. This night is beautiful too, the bus has broken down in the middle of nowhere and we are not even bothered to reach home. Look at others, and how tense they are, we are so happy being lost.

Farhan :

Maybe because being lost is a special feeling, until you are not lost you cannot find yourself. It's beautiful to be lost.

Sarthak :

Now I feel a desperate urge to light my cigarette to wake me up. I want a lighter,

(surprisingly no one had one, the mechanic gave him a match)

Farhan :

It's funny how a couple is trying to resolve a fight to find something they had lost, another man on the bus was looking for Digene for his stomach ache, a woman was looking for her kids pamper kit, you are looking for a lighter, there was one lady she was finding a place to pee,........

And that man standing in between the road to stop a bus to get into the bus, he said he would need some rubber strap to get the bus started and he couldn't find the spare one in the bus. Each one here is looking for something, and you're looking for a lighter. In the course of events, we are all looking for something. And how important is what we are looking for only depends on us. For the Lady to find a place to pee is as important as finding the rubber strap to get the bus started and as important as for the couple to resolve their bitterness. Amidst all this, here I am just talking to you, not bothered when we will reach......

After some moments of spending time together, the bus strap is fixed and the bus finally starts they both go in,

Sarthak :

(these are thoughts and he is talking to himself) The sky overhead is filled with stars and millions of crickets are chirping. I could hear his breath, like a blue breeze. I fell asleep listening to it flow.

Slowly the bus starts.

Music - Stars Die by Porcupine can be played here from the last few stanzas until the scenes fade to the next.

Scene VI
The Dawn

Farhan :

(these are thoughts and he is talking to himself) See Jesus will show us the way and this is how he might be showing us the way, I have been in the Paulo buses so many times it has never broken down, and today when I meet such an amazing person it does. Is it coincidence but it cannot be that coincidental? Coincidences, Borders of

Love.......Longing.

There is a certain quantitative border that must not be crossed, yet no one ever realizes that it exists. And in this moment, I've crossed this border, not knowing what is to come......... Is it all because of this Love, this night, this journey, the bus, Sarthak, Berth No 15, Ukulele or what exactly? How did this unveil?

Maybe Love is love, that's all you can say about it. It's a pair of wings beating in my heart and driving me to do things that seem unwise.......

Farhan :

(these are thoughts and he is talking to himself) He was resting on my arms, and I didn't feel like waking him or even moving an inch. He was asleep like a baby in a castle of glass that would shatter in a single blow. So, I let him rest in that fragile moment. Not being

able to fall asleep anymore and not allowing myself to move, I had become one with this berth: maybe 'the love berth'

Farhan moved the curtain a little and looked outside.

It was still dark but in one instant the horizon became a faint line suspended in the darkness and then the line was drawn upward, higher and higher. It was as if a giant hand had stretched down from the sky and slowly lifted the curtain of night from the face of the earth.......

Farhan :

(these are thoughts and he is talking to himself) The sun was gleaming and all I knew was that in a few moments, we would disappear like dew drops in the morning sun.

Farhan's heart is pounding as he knows it will be 7 am soon and he might never meet him. Will Sarthak disappear? He can't call, he does not have a phone; or a number! Of course, there is Facebook but people do get lost. He kept wondering 'Why did it happen at all if it just had to be just one night?'

Farhan :

(these are thoughts and he is talking to himself) Why did it strike the chords of my heart? Why–did it happen when I came so far from home? Why did somebody find a key to my heart? Just like Murakami's books people come and disappear in some strange land. Will this night be a dream? Will it be only thoughts that play in my mind? If I never meet him again who

knows what will happen, who knows how things will end…

Lights dim to blue

Scene VII
The Tinted Glass

Sarthak gives up his Ukulele and goes to drop him down. Sarthak hugs him tight, they hug each other tight, and to hide their emotions they put on their sunglasses at 7 in the morning. They feel the pain of separation. After the tight hug, he gets on the bus and the bus moves away. He tries to see Sarthak from the tainted black windows, but Sarthak disappears in the darkness. Farhan walks home (into the audience) with the sunshine, and he wonders if it was all a dream, but it was not a dream. Because he has a Ukulele in his hand that shows it had happened. It was not a dream. That there was a night like this once upon a time.

Farhan :

(these are thoughts and he is talking to himself) The bus door that led to Sarthak's, would have slammed shut behind me and I needed to find my bearings in a new and different one.

Sarthak :

(these are thoughts and he is talking to himself) Once he got out of the bus and was gone, my world was suddenly hollow and meaningless. I'm now feeling like a snail without a shell. I feel scared about this lonely berth and how I will spend the remaining journey.

Farhan :

(these are thoughts and he is talking to himself) I had my little world within me. A world that was for me alone, none could enter. That's how I was protecting it. I let him 'in' and now the world has changed. Why do I feel, if I never see him again, I will go insane?

Sarthak :

(these are thoughts and he is talking to himself) The night disappeared. It seemed as if a poet were writing his greatest poem with ink that instantly disappears.

Music - Fly On by Cold Play can be played here

Curtain

About the Author

Dr. Omkar Bhatkar is a Sociologist with a doctoral thesis concerned with Proxemics and Social Ecology. He has been a visiting professor for a decade now teaching Film Theory, Culture Studies, and Gender Studies. He has also served as a faculty for the London School of Economics International Programmes in Sociology.

He is the Co-Founder and Head of the eclectic 'St. Andrew's Centre for Philosophy and Performing Arts which constantly strives to bridge art and academics. Dr. Omkar Bhatkar runs his own theatre group known as Metamorphosis Theatre Inc. His works largely focus on Poetry in Motion, Existentialist Themes, and Contemporary French Plays in Translation. He has written and directed more than twenty plays, several of which have been performed at

Art and Theatre Festivals. In collaboration with Alliance Française de Bombay, he has directed several Contemporary French Plays in English. He is also a Stage Critic and reviews plays. Dr Bhatkar's play 'Blue Storm' was selected at the Asia Playwrights Theatre Festival 2021 held in South Korea. 'Blue Storm' was also an invitation play at the International Women's Theatre Festival 2021 held in Incheon, South Korea. Though he is grounded in theatre, he also explores the world of films. As a filmmaker, he has written and directed independent feature films like Perhaps Tea, The Farewell Band, Testament of Emily, and also a poetic documentary titled 'Painted Hymns: The Chapels of Santa Monica'. Recently, he made an experimental feature film titled 'Time, Distance, Memory on the Feather of a Wing'

He is a thalassophile who finds solace by drowning in the depths of poetry and spends his waking life painting, reading, writing, and engaging in conversations over black tea.

www.ingramcontent.com/pod-product-compliance
Lightning Source LLC
LaVergne TN
LVHW041635070526
838199LV00052B/3383